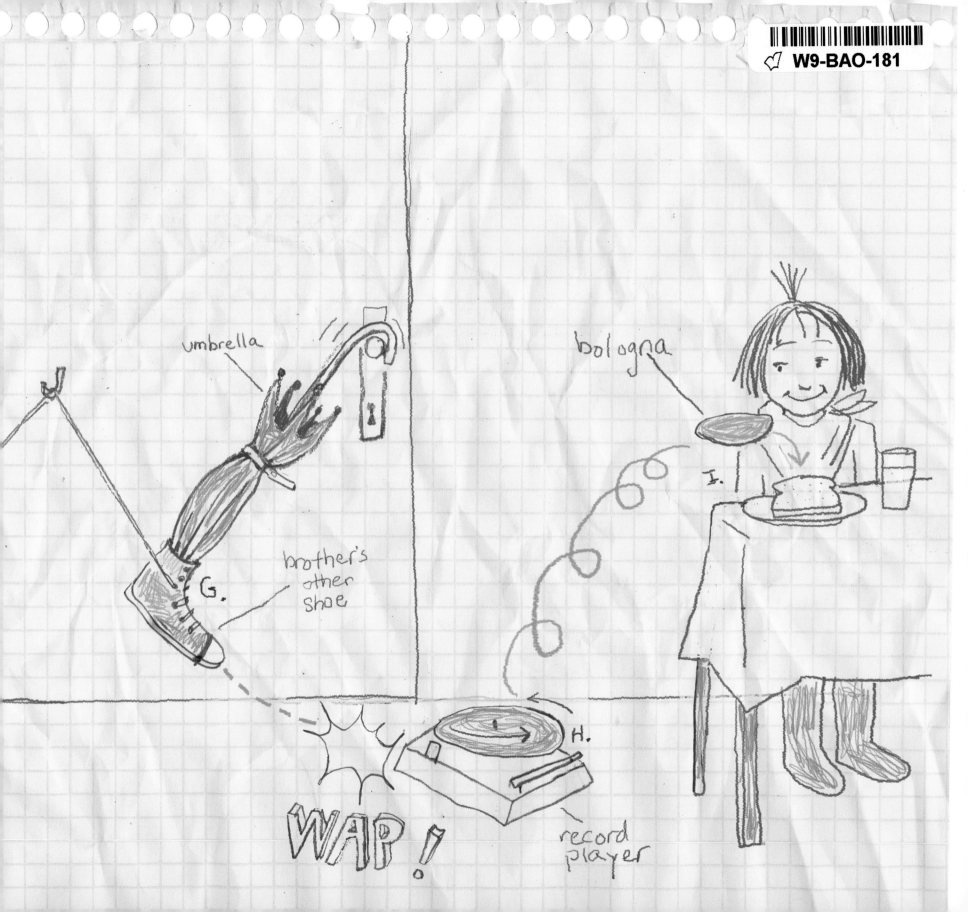

For Theodora
—J.O.

For Anne and Lee
—N.C.

Visit us on the Web! www.randomhouse.com/kids
Educators and librarians, for a variety of teaching tools, visit us at www.randomhouse.com/teachers

Library of Congress Cataloging-in-Publication Data
Offill, Jenny.
11 experiments that failed / by Jenny Offill; pictures by Nancy Carpenter.—1st ed.
p. cm.
Summary: A young child tries a series of wacky experiments, such as seeing if a piece of
bologna will fly like a Frisbee and determining whether seedlings will grow if watered with
expensive perfume, and then must suffer the consequences of experiments gone awry.
ISBN 978-0-375-84762-2 (trade) — ISBN 978-0-375-95762-8 (glb)
— ISBN 978-0-375-98384-9 (ebook)
[1. Experiments—Fiction. 2. Humorous stories.] I. Carpenter, Nancy, ill. II. Title.
III. Title: Eleven experiments that failed.
PZ7.O3277Aaf 2011
[E]—dc22
2009045096

The text of this book is set in Regula.
The illustrations were rendered in pen-and-ink and digital media.
Book design by Rachael Cole

MANUFACTURED IN CHINA
16
First Edition

11 Experiments That Failed

written by JENNY OFFILL   pictures by NANCY CARPENTER

schwartz & wade books · new york

EXPERIMENTS WITH FOOD

Question:

Can a kid make it through the winter eating only snow and ketchup?

Hypothesis:

Ketchup and snow are the only food groups a kid needs.

What You Need:

- Ketchup
- Snow

150 ml

100

50

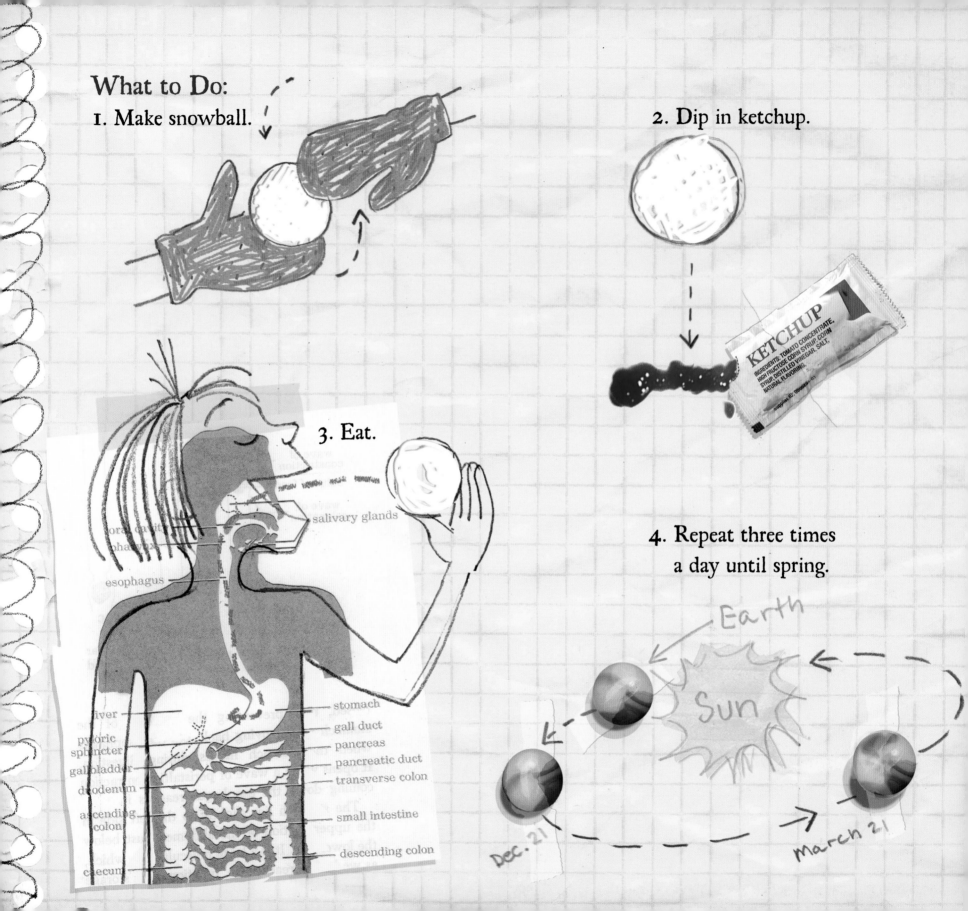

What Happened:
- Stomachache.
- Brain freeze.
- Love of ketchup wavering.

Question:
What makes fungus grow?

Hypothesis:
If left in a closet, food will rot and become a colorful fungus garden.

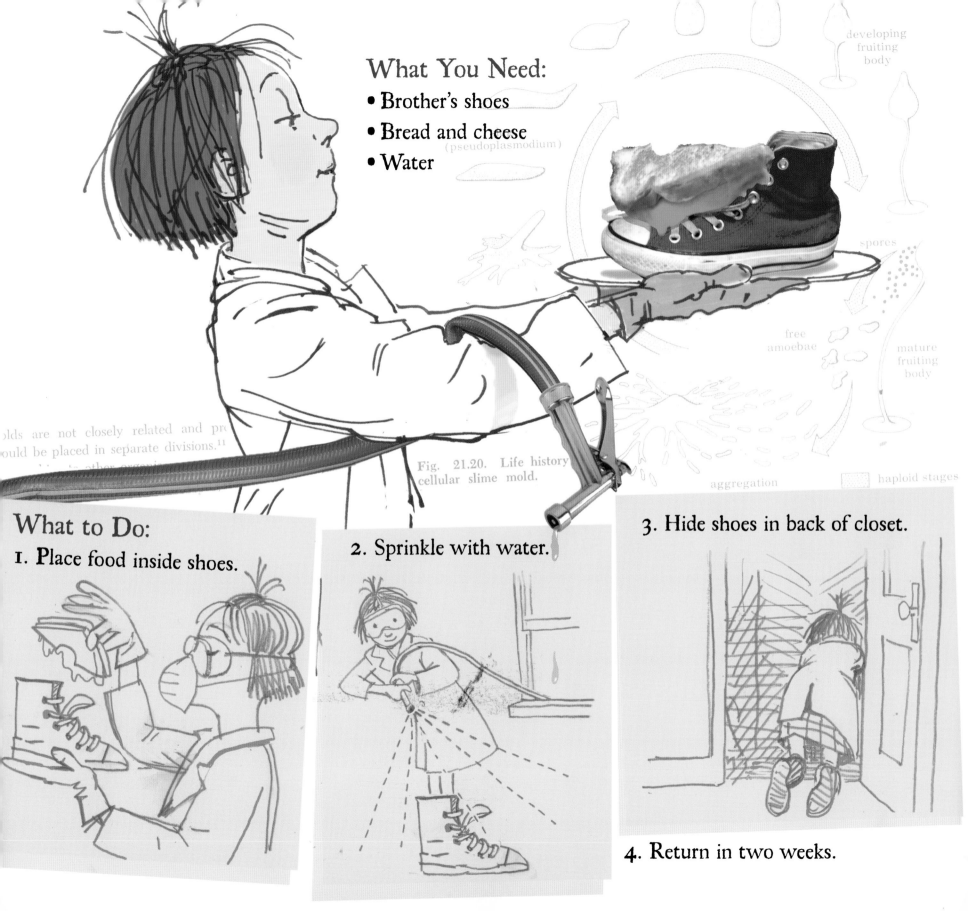

What You Need:
- Brother's shoes
- Bread and cheese
- Water

developing fruiting body

(pseudoplasmodium)

spores

free amoebae

mature fruiting body

...olds are not closely related and pr... ...ould be placed in separate divisions.[11]

Fig. 21.20. Life history cellular slime mold.

aggregation

haploid stages

What to Do:
1. Place food inside shoes.

2. Sprinkle with water.

3. Hide shoes in back of closet.

4. Return in two weeks.

What Happened:
Experiment still under way.

EXPERIMENTS WITH ANIMALS

Question:

Would gerbils like bigger wheels?

Hypothesis:

Gerbils would like bigger wheels.

What You Need:
- Gerbil
- Ferris wheel

What to Do:
1. Take gerbil to amusement park.

2. Strap gerbil into seat with you.

3. Hold gerbil's paw.

4. Go around and around and around.

What Happened:
Gerbil not allowed on ride.
(Too short.)

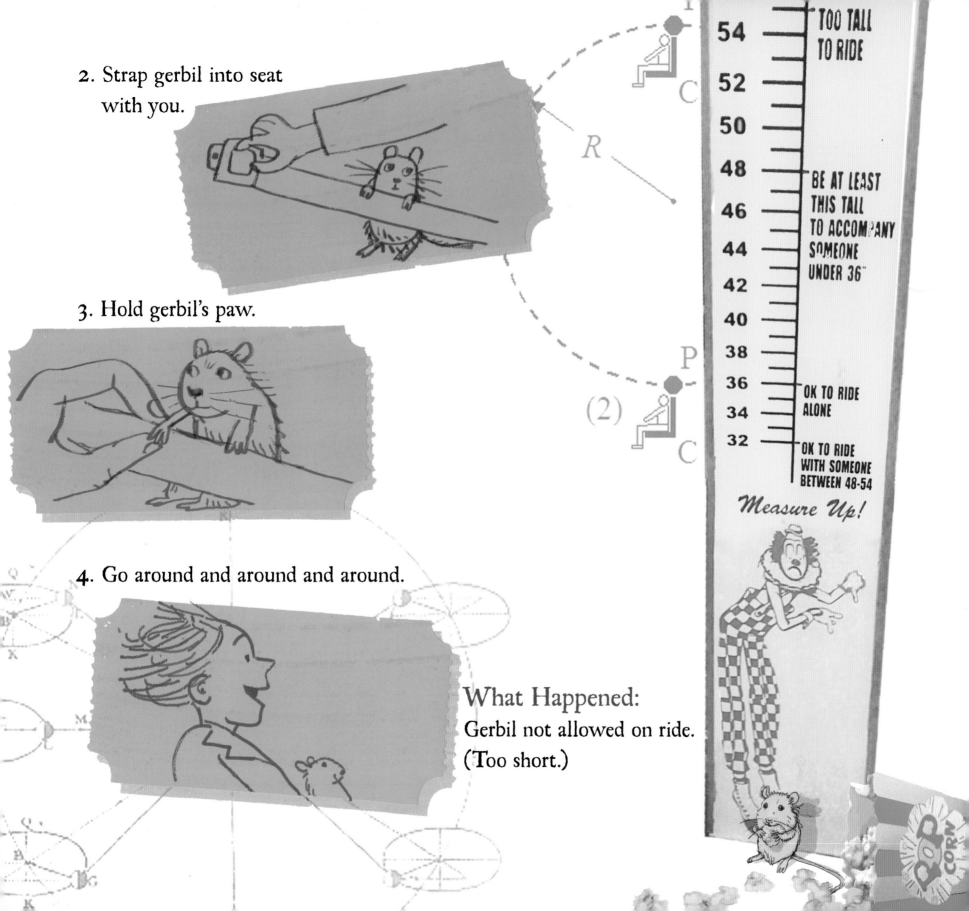

54
52
50
48
46
44
42
40
38
36
34
32

TOO TALL
TO RIDE

BE AT LEAST
THIS TALL
TO ACCOMPANY
SOMEONE
UNDER 36"

OK TO RIDE
ALONE

OK TO RIDE
WITH SOMEONE
BETWEEN 48-54

Measure Up!

POP CORN

Question:
Do dogs like to be covered in glitter?

Hypothesis:
Dogs like everything.

What You Need:
• Dog
• Tube of glitter

What to Do:

1. Call dog.

2. Cover with glitter.

3. Let dog go.

What Happened:
- Dog ate glitter.
- Pink sparkly yard.

Question:
Can a live beaver be ordered
through the mail?

Hypothesis:
A live beaver can be ordered
through the mail.

What You Need:
- Five-dollar bill
- Envelope
- Stamp

What to Do:

I. Fill out mail-order beaver form.

2. Attach five-dollar bill.

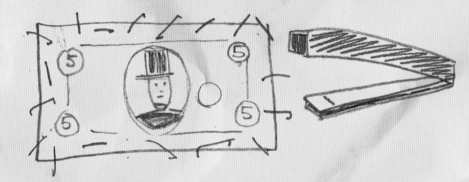

3. Place form in stamped envelope.

4. Mail.

What Happened:

- Allowance withheld until further notice.
- House declared No Beaver zone.

EXPERIMENTS WITH MOTION

Question:

What is the best way to speed up a boring car ride?

Hypothesis:

Yodeling makes time go faster.

What You Need:

- One adult
- Three children
- Traffic jam

30 feet

takeoff point

25 feet

What to Do:

1. Yell "Yodelayheehoo."

2. Yell "Yodelayheehoo" even louder.

3. Repeat as needed.

Velocity (m s⁻¹)

10
9
8
7
6
5
4
3
2
1
0

0 1 2 3 4 5 6 7 8 9 10 11

Time (s)

What Happened:
- Walked to school.
- Felt lonesome like a cowboy.

Question:

Will a piece of bologna fly like a Frisbee?

Hypothesis:

A piece of bologna will fly like a Frisbee.

What You Need:
- Bologna

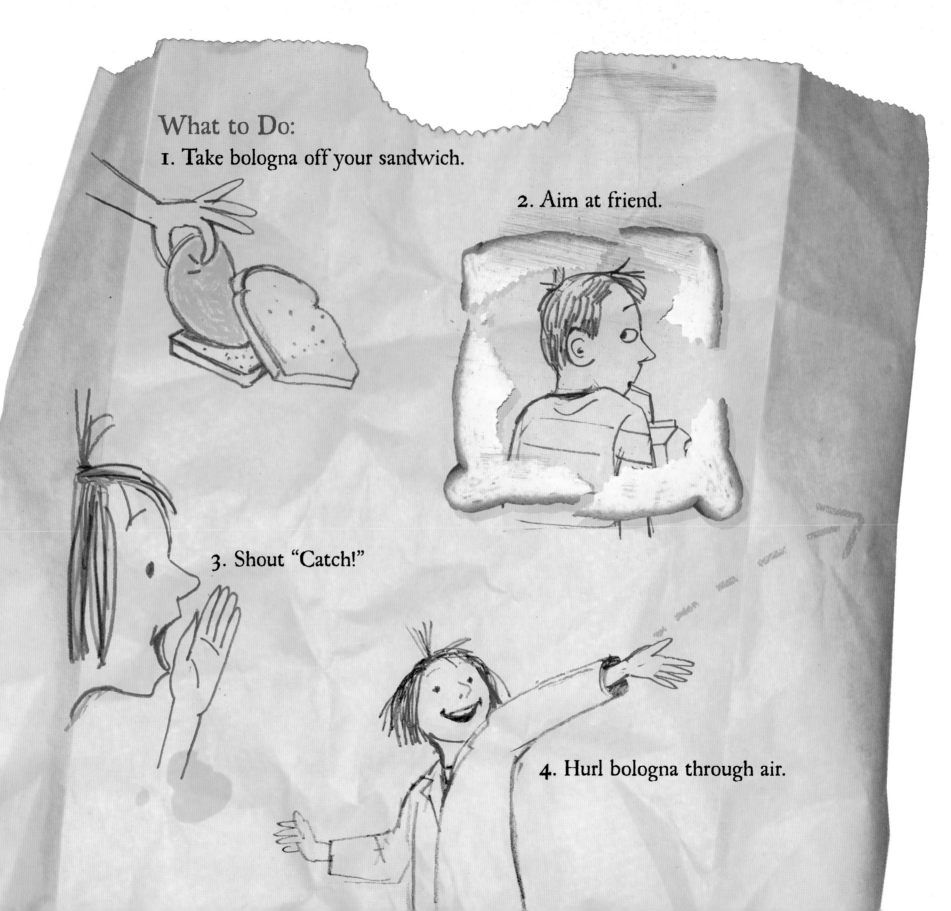

What to Do:

1. Take bologna off your sandwich.

2. Aim at friend.

3. Shout "Catch!"

4. Hurl bologna through air.

What Happened:
- Teacher caught bologna with his head.
- No recess.

EXPERIMENTS WITH PERFUME

O_2

Question:
Will seedlings grow if given Eau La La instead of water?

Hypothesis:
Seedlings will like Eau La La better than water.

CO_2

H_2O Eau La La

What You Need:
- Pots
- Dirt
- Seedlings
- Water
- Fancy perfume

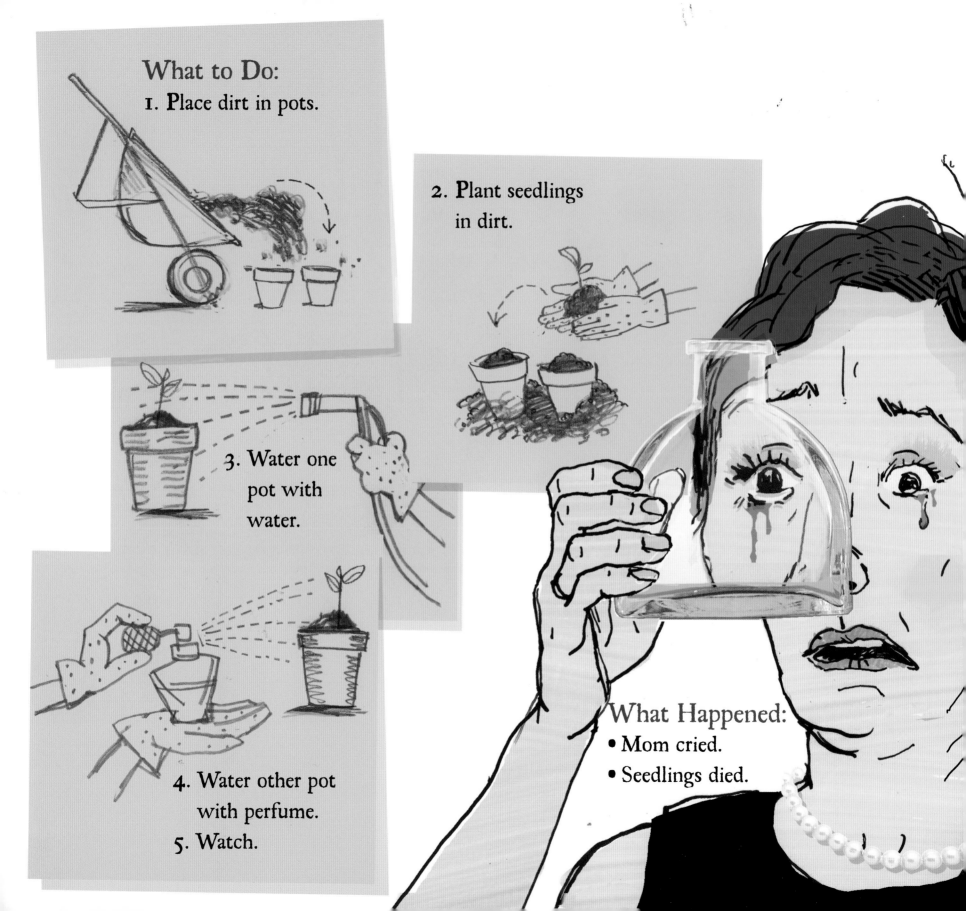

What to Do:

1. Place dirt in pots.

2. Plant seedlings in dirt.

3. Water one pot with water.

4. Water other pot with perfume.

5. Watch.

What Happened:
- Mom cried.
- Seedlings died.

Question:
Is there a way to make stinky cheese smell better?

Hypothesis:
Perfume will make stinky cheese smell better.

What You Need:
- Fancy perfume
- Stinky cheese

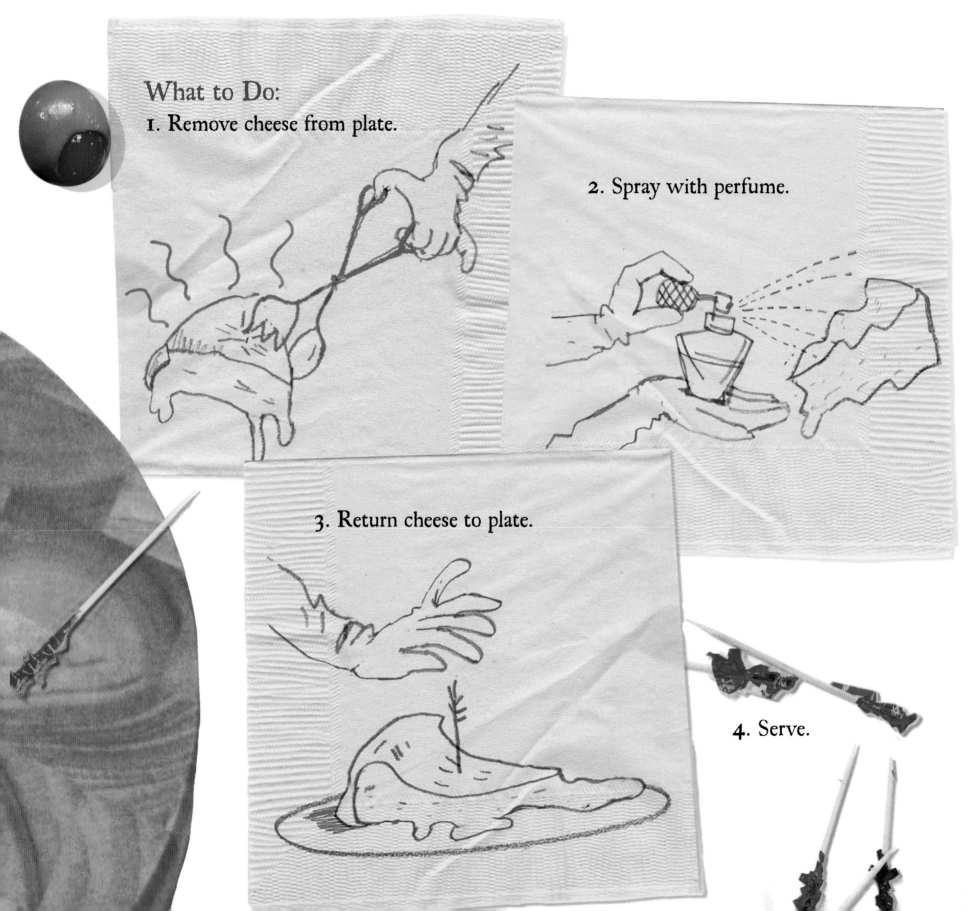

What to Do:

1. Remove cheese from plate.

2. Spray with perfume.

3. Return cheese to plate.

4. Serve.

What Happened:
- Unhappy guests.
- Leftovers.

EXPERIMENTS WITH HOUSEHOLD OBJECTS

Question:
Can a washing machine wash dishes?

Hypothesis:
A washing machine can wash anything.

What You Need:
- Washing machine
- Dirty dishes

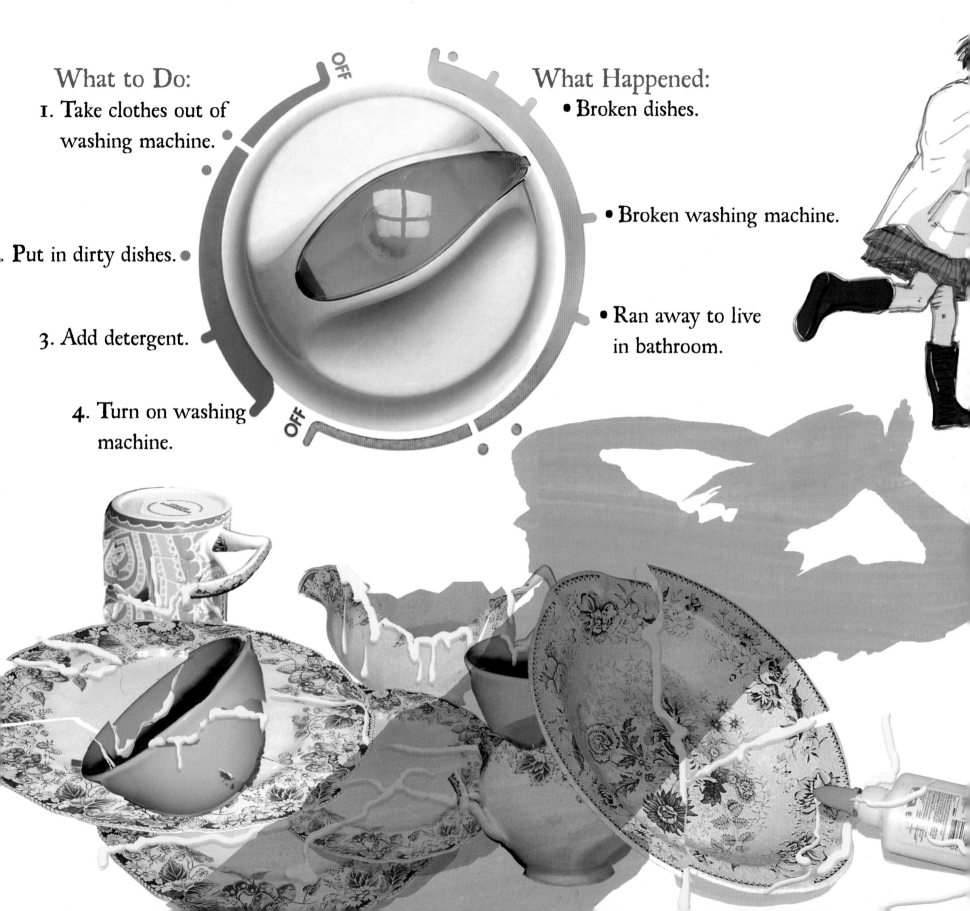

What to Do:

1. Take clothes out of washing machine.

2. Put in dirty dishes.

3. Add detergent.

4. Turn on washing machine.

What Happened:

- Broken dishes.

- Broken washing machine.

- Ran away to live in bathroom.

Question:
Can a message be sent in a bottle to a faraway land?

Hypothesis:
The hole in the bottom of the toilet leads to the sea.

What You Need:
- Message
- Bottle
- Toilet

What Happened:
- Toilet overflowed.
- Plumber called.
- Still awaiting rescue.

A.

B.

C.

D.

E.

F.

H.